why why why
pourquoi perché proč dlaczego hvorfor warum waarom niçin çür nach yıarı pam

For Laura. Why? It just is – L.C.
For Abigail and Penguin – T.R.

Text copyright © 1998 by Lindsay Camp. Illustrations copyright © 1998 by Tony Ross.

The rights of Lindsay Camp and Tony Ross to be identified as the author and illustrator of this work
have been asserted by them in accordance with the Copyright, Designs and Patents Act, 1988.

First published in Great Britain in 1998 by Andersen Press Ltd., 20 Vauxhall Bridge Road, London SW1V 2SA.
Published in Australia by Random House Australia Pty., 20 Alfred Street, Milsons Point, Sydney, NSW 2061.
All rights reserved. Colour separated in Switzerland by Photolitho AG, Offsetreproduktionen, Gossau, Zürich.
Printed and bound in Italy by Grafiche AZ, Verona.

10   9   8   7   6   5   4   3   2   1

British Library Cataloguing in Publication Data available.

ISBN 0 86264 793 2

*This book has been printed on acid-free paper*

written by Lindsay Camp
illustrated by Tony Ross

A

Andersen Press
London

There was one thing Lily did that drove her dad mad.

Actually, it wasn't a thing she *did*.

It was a thing she said.

She said it all the time.

She said it first thing in the morning.

It's time you were dressed.

Why?

She said it at breakfast time.

Your egg just needs another minute.

Why?

She said it when they went shopping.

Mustn't forget to buy some more bin bags.

Why?

She said it when her dad read her a story.

And, of course, she said it at bedtime.

Usually, Lily's dad did his best to explain.

Because it rained all
last night.

Why?

Because there
were lots of big
black clouds full of
tiny drops of water.

Why?

Because . . . well, there
just were, Lily.

There just
were!

But sometimes, when he was a bit tired or too busy,

he'd just get cross.

Then, one Friday, something rather unusual happened.

Lily was playing in the sandpit in the park.

Suddenly, Lily's dad stopped and looked upwards. So did Lily.
And so did everybody else in the park.

Lily was too astonished to say anything. After all, she'd never seen
a gigantic Thargon spaceship before.

The Thargon spaceship came lower, and then it landed in the park, right next to the sandpit.

Everybody stood and stared. The doors of the spaceship slid open

and out squelched several Thargons.

They didn't look very friendly.

The most important Thargon oozed forward.

Everyone started to tremble.

Everyone except Lily, that is.

Why?

**WHY?**
Because that is our
mission, of course.

Why?

Because destroying
puny planets brings
glory to the mighty
Thargon Empire.

Why?

Because . . . well,
because our Great Leader,
the Imperial Tharg, says so.

Why?

Because . . . he just does,
Small Female Earthling,
he just does. Hmmm . . .

The chief Thargon turned to his friends. He looked thoughtful.

Lily and her dad and all the other people watched as they talked together in Thargish for quite a long time.

Then the chief Thargon slithered forward again, and spoke to Lily.

Lily was just about to say something

but her dad put his hand over her mouth,

just in time.

That night at bedtime, when he'd finished reading her a story,

Lily's dad gave her an extra big hug.

And then he promised he'd never get cross with her again,
no matter how often she asked him why.

I was very proud
of you in the park
today.

Why?

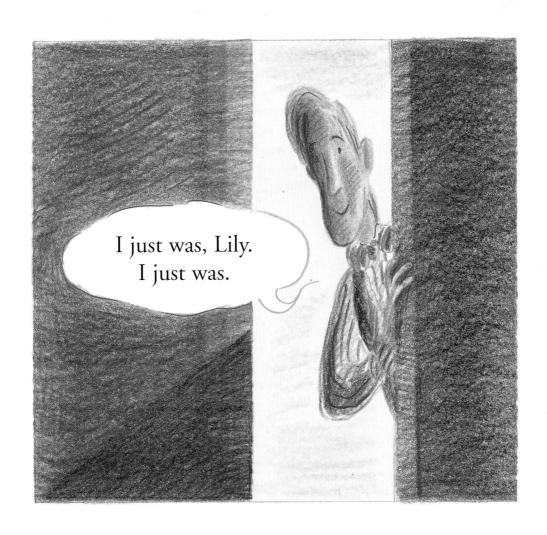

why Pourquoi Waarom TXT nach Pourquoi why? Per
vari warum nach Perché?
为什么 hvorfor hvorfor 为什么? 为什么? wa
Proč hvorfor Proč Proč Perché
Pourquoi nach nach Proč
Pourquoi Waarum Proč TXT Porque Perché
Waarum cur why TXT Proč dlaczego hvorfor niçin Pourquoi
Why niçin why?
niçin warum why Proč
ISLS why nacyr ? ISLS ? Pourquoi why
Proč niçin niçin perqué
为什么 why niçin yiarí hvorfor ? cur Pour
thy Pourquoi why TXT nach nach ? cur why
vari ? niçin Proč Pour que Pourquoi Pourquoi niçin
ISLS nach why
niçin Pourquoi hvorfor niçin
Pam perqué cur why
为什么 dlaczego Pourquoi why 为什么
ISLS why Proč nach Pourquoi hvorfor ISLS N
Why Pourquoi Proč why yiarí Perqué поч
warum hvorfor Pam
hvorfor niçin nach yiarí why Waarum vari
perqué why Почему TXT Perqué why Pam
为什么 dlaczego Pam Pourquoi niçin niçin
why Pourquoi cur